OUT THE MUD

BY

KAREEM

OUT THE MUD

Copyright © 2020 by KAREEM

Printed in the U.S.A 1st Edition

Paperback ISBN: 978-1-7358550-7-3

Library Of Congress

Veenus Publishing
+1-847-904-0352
Highland, Indiana

www.shenalvee.com

DEDICATION

I dedicate this book to my pops,
Wallace Brown Jr (R.I.P), and my mom
Frances Brown; thank you for the life lessons
and for allowing me to spread my wings and
fly.

OUT THE MUD

CHAPTER ONE

After driving for thirteen hours straight, I pulled into my Grandmothers' dusty driveway; it's been a few years since I was here. I finished unloading my possessions from the trailer. "Finally!" I exasperated, sitting down in an old rocking chair on my granny's weather-beaten porch. A funny meme from my little brother came through and made me laugh—watching the tall, weeded grass sway as if it's saying welcome home. I take the last sip of iced tea, reminiscing on the many summers I've spent here as a kid. I still can't believe a month has gone by since she died.

A green SUV stops in front of the house, snapping me out of my daze. I see a beautiful, high yella' older woman gets out of the car smiling.

"Hi, are you Quincy?"

Stepping off the porch, "Yes, ma'am!"

"I'm Helen Taylor. I'm a friend of your grandmothers; you probably don't remember me."

"Yes, I remember you, ma'am!" I retorted. Helen is the pastor's wife and dubbed the town's gossiper. I've been checking her out on social media for years now. She teaches yoga and does workout videos. She is very fit to be in her mid-sixties, I'm talking abs *and* legs. "Welcome back to town! You are even more handsome than the last time I saw you!"

Blushing, "thank you, I try!" laughing, "You look nice as well, Mrs. Taylor. I said to myself, who is this fine woman, stopping!" Mrs. Taylor can most definitely get the business. "Oh, stop it!" She says, smiling from ear to ear. Her cheeks turned beet red; I guess she was flattered by the compliment. "I know you just got here, and you are probably hungry!"

"Yes, ma'am, I'm famished!"

"Well, I'm having a fish fry tonight at the house. If you would like to stop by, we'll be more than happy to have you."

"Ok, that sounds good. What time should I come, Mrs. Taylor?"

"Say about around six, baby. Give me your telephone number so that I can text you the address."

After giving her my cell number, "Thank you! Should I bring something?"

"No, honey, I have plenty of everything!" "I will see you later then!"

"Ok! Quincy," waving as she was getting inside the car.

"Dammit!" I damn near get electrocuted trying to turn on the breaker box for-the air conditioner. Man, this shit is old as hell; it's going to take me all day to figure this mess out! "Thank you, Nana, for leaving me this mess," I groan, looking towards the sky. Fuck this! I'm going to facetime my dad.

"Hey, son, what's going on?

"Dad, I can't seem to figure out this old ass breaker box. I blew a fuse turning on the air conditioner." Turning the phone towards it. "You see the blue fuse on your left?" He asked.

"Yeah, I see it." "Untwist it, Quincy."

"Ok, dad, I did it."

"That's the size fuse you need. That breaker box hasn't been improved since your grandparents brought the house." "I can see that."

"Cool, I'm about to run to the store before I go to the Taylor's for a fish fry."

"Be careful, son, that nigga Earl is slippery as a snake."

"Oh, I remember, dad. I'm watching him."

"He tried to swindle your Nana plenty of times. He's still mad; I took your mama from him."

"Because my daddy got that game!"

"You damn right, I do." Like father, like son.

"Ok, Dad, I will call you later."

"Say hi to Helen for me; And go by your Aunt Pam's house; I don't feel like hearing her mouth," my dad reminded.

My daddy was Helen's first, and I had overheard him once talking when he was drunk, saying she was a wild animal in the bed. He was going to marry her but met my mother when she attended college down here.

CHAPTER TWO

Driving down a dirt road, I can hear the tiny pebbles hitting the undercarriage. This fucking dust has gotten my Cadillac SUV dirtier than a motherfucker, reminding me exactly why I didn't want to live in the south. I arrived at the address Helen had given me. I remember this house; they've since added additions to it. Music is playing from the speakers, and kids are playing in the yard. A group of men is huddled around the outdoor fryer, drinking beer. I see some women sitting under a canopy tent, enjoying their cocktails. I took one last pull from my Newport before getting out of the truck. As I made my way up to the house, Mrs. Taylor greets me.

"Glad you could make it, Quincy." Hugging me. I can tell she has been drinking by the flirtatious hug and the butt pat. "Boy, You look just like your fine ass daddy!" she let out a slight giggle.

"Thank you again for inviting me." She smelled like fried fish mixed with baby powder.

"Come on, handsome." Interlocking her arm with mine, "Let me introduce you to everybody. Hey, everyone, this is Daisy's grandson Quincy!"

Mr. Taylor walks up to me, extending his hand. "Hey, Quincy, it has been a while since I last saw you, son. Boy, have you grown. looking like your daddy."

"What's going on, Mr. Taylor? I see you have added a few things to the house since I was last here."

"Yes, son, God has been good to us." Mr. Taylor responded proudly.

"All the time." Mrs. Taylor chimes in, still holding on to my arm. Pastor Taylor looks troubled. I'm not going to pay him any mind though. I know the history between him and my dad; he doesn't want any smoke with my Pops.

While drinking with a few of the fellas, we talked about sports, and since I am from Chicago, I had to represent the crib. I notice a Chevy Denali truck with these huge ass rims approaching, roaring up the street. I finally see who it is; it's my cousin, Terrance, banging loud music. My grandmother has spoken to me numerous times on the phone about Terrance. My Auntie had gotten a substantial 8-figure settlement after her husband died in a fire on his job a couple of years back. She told me he likes spending his money on them fast tail gals. "What's up, Q!" he greeted me with a hug. "What up, Terrance! It's good to see you, cousin."

"So, you moved down here for good, huh?" "Yeah, I'm trying to see what this southern life is all about." Plus, I needed a change of scenery after getting laid off from the airline.

"That's what's up, cousin. We're going to turn up the Evansville way a little later, on me." he inferred.

"That's a bet! I will most definitely take you up on your offer, big dawg," laughing, as we hugged.

"Cool. We are going to see if your ass ready, my boy! I'm about to go say hi to everyone, talk to you in a minute," Terrance hints as he walks away.

Later that evening, playing spades with Mr. Taylor and a few other people. A woman walks up, "Hi, Daddy!" kissing Mr. Taylor on the cheek. She is stunning! Honey complexion and these amazing hazel-colored eyes. Showing off her curves in a pair of black leggings and a yellow t-shirt that reads 'Brown Women Are The Future.'

Mr. Taylor was smiling, "Aww, baby, you made it."

Damn, that's Denise! I start checking for a ring, and I don't see one. Now, I'm really eager.

"How was the conference?" Mr., Taylor asks Denise.

"It was excellent, daddy."

"Good! Good! Did you get to see your brother while you were in Atlanta?"

"Yes!" Rustling through her oversized bag. "He sent you this." Handing him a bottle of moonshine.

"That's my boy!" turning, looking at me, beaming, "Hey, Denise, you remember Quincy, don't you, Daisy's grandson?"

"Yes, she talked about him all the time. I'm sorry about your nana; we certainly lost an angel; she was a very sagacious woman." Shaking her hand, it was soft and firm "thank you, Denise, she spoke of you often too."

"Where's mom, daddy?"

"She's over there running her mouth as usual." they both chuckled as she stepped away. "Hey, Quincy, do you remember Denise?" Denise was my down south summer's fling, the first girl I kissed, hell the first girl that played with my manhood. She and I used to direct message each other on social media. We had lost touch, and I haven't spoken to her in three years. I'm going to see what's up what her. I'm trying to see about that situation; I'm talking about that caboose.

"Yes, I do!" With my eyes on her as she stood next to her mother. And I notice her looking at me as well.

Terrance interrupts the conversation patting me on the shoulder, "Come, take a ride with me, cousin."

Excusing myself from the table, "It was nice of you to invite me out. I will be back to do this again." smiling, hugging Mrs. Taylor.

Mr. Taylor approaches his wife, Mrs. Taylor, asking, "Hey, what was with that show you were putting on? You were all arm and arm with that kid?"

"That was nothing, Earl. He's a good boy. I was giving him a welcome, trying to make him feel at home."

Well, I think he is trouble like his daddy and his Pawpaw. Stay away from him, and don't make me repeat it, Helen." Mr. Taylor commands.

"Oh, is somebody jealous after all the bullshit I've put up with?"

Grabbing her, sternly, "Not tonight!" Snatching away from him, "Your little game doesn't work anymore, Earl, you have more to lose. Remember, it's my daddy's land that church sits on, so make that the last time you put your hands on me, snake.

CHAPTER THREE

As Terrance and I rode through town, you can hear the train wheels crackling along the tracks. We pass by the gas station, slash drive- thru liquor store. I take in the scene, and all I can think of is how country this motherfucker is. There's a group of people out front congregating. The shit looks like something from a rap video. My guess this is the strip. Terrance turns up the music before lighting up a blunt, slowing down so everyone can see him, "You smoke, Q?"

"Hell yeah, I smoke; not that reg though."

"Boy, you tripping, I only blow that gas."

"I heard y'all blow that dirt down here." Laughing.

"Whoever told you that bullshit is a lie." Terrance retorted, standing on his product, "Damn! It's some hoes out here tonight." blowing his horn at some females dancing on top of a car. He starts yelling, "Yeah, shake that thang!"

As we smoked and rode, he was giving me the rundown on all the townspeople. Midway through us talking, "Terrance, what's up with Denise?" I asked.

"Cuz, fuck that stuck up ass broad! Denise acts like she's too good for the men around here."

She's the town's council president and runs the town's youth center.

We pull into the parking lot of this hole in the wall bar. From the neon sign on the roof, I can tell it's a booty club. As we enter the establishment, naked women are dancing on the pole and giving lap dances. While other women are walking around, trying to find a trick. Not usually my scene, but fuck it, since I'm here, I might as well enjoy myself. We sat at the bar drinking a bottle of Gentlemen's Jack, burning big gas. In the south, smoking indoors is acceptable, not like in Chicago. My cousin is throwing a large stack of five-dollar bills at these two thick women dancing in front of us.

"Q, do you want to go into the back room? "The backroom! Say cuz; I'm not with all that freaky shit." We laughed.

"Boy, I'm talking about the VIP. You can take any one of these chicks or hell both, fuck it. My treat."

"Man, cuz, I'm high, tipsy, and horny, I want both of them."

"Do you! Have fun, my boy!"

I slide in their ears. I was putting that Chi-Town lingo down. They're laughing and giggling, agreeing to let me hit both of them. I pour myself another glass of whiskey. "I will be back, Terrance. I am about to go and shift these hoes kidneys, cuz." I said, smiling devilishly.

"Both them hoes got that lake and sloppy toppy, Q!"

Before leaving with the strippers, "Say cuz, you got some rubbers?"

"Yeah, cuz, I got you!" as he is passing me a few Magnum condoms and giving each of the women cash and a small pack of ecstasy pills. "Say Q, I'm going to be around here somewhere, you good bro, nobody is going to fuck with you."

I am starting to realize that Terrance sells drugs. I should've known because of the way he moves, just like my little brother. Dapping Terrance up, "good looking, cuz."

I see this sexy slim redbone with red micro braids punch some dude in the face.

Terrance is shaking his head, "this girl here." "You straight, Terrance?" I asked

"Yeah, I'm good. Go fuck something; I got this."

"Say less." disappearing with both women into the back.

Inside the room was a large black leather couch against the wall and a wooden round table with red lights. I guess to set the mood. The girls began kissing and rubbing on each other; the pills must've kicked in. One of the women is named Cinnamon. She's milk chocolate with a fat ass and has her clit and nipples pierced. She initiates the action by massaging my dick as I'm smoking. The other one is named Honey. She's a caramel complexion baddie with tattoos that cover her body from the neck down. Honey takes my shirt off and starts kissing my neck and rubbing on my chest. I get lost in the intoxicating smell of her perfume. "Damn, that feels good, baby."

"You like that, huh, Big Daddy?"

"Take these motherfucking pants off!" Cinnamon demanded as she pulls them off along with my boxers.

"Damn, daddy, you got a log!" Referring to the size of my shit.

She then slides a condom on my dick and starts bobbing me slowly. I lean my head over and begin flicking my tongue on Vanilla's nipple ring while fingering her slowly. That box soggy and tight. My dick is at full attention after Cinnamon's mouth bath. Cinnamon then stands and straddles me cowgirl style. Man, her pussy was wetter than a raindrop, so wet that my thighs were soaked in her juices. Cinnamon leans back on my stomach and chest. Honey gets down on her knees and proceeds to give both of us oral stimulation.

"Shit!" her pussy has tightened around my dick. I knew she was about to cum. She is springing up and down, saying, "Fuck me, don't stop! I'm about to!" screaming out in pleasure. A rush of water exited her, right into Honey's face. We got a squirter.

"I want some of that fat ass dick!" Honey whispered in my ear as she bends over the couch, twerking her ass. I'm standing up, sliding into her, my hands were around her waist, I'm balls deep pounding her. She is loudly moaning, her face is in between Cinnamon's legs, "Yes, daddy, I feel you in my stomach! I'm about to Cum!" Dam! It seemed like lotion was flowing out of her.

An hour later, we emerged from the back, smiling like chess cats. Both women kissed me on the cheeks. "Come back and see us." I exchanged numbers with Honey for a session later on down the road.

"You ready to go, cuz?"

"Yeah, cuz!" Feeling like a million bucks and refreshed after a good sex session, it's been a few weeks since I had some.

A Spanish chick walks up out of nowhere and hands Terrance a wad of money. Terrance stuffs it in his pockets, saying, "Let's go before these motherfuckers in here jump stupid!" He drove me back to my car, and the Spanish chick rode with us. My guess, he is about to go have his own session.

29

CHAPTER FOUR

The next afternoon, I'm sweating bullets while riding the mower, trying to get this yard together. This Florida heat is on my ass. It's hotter than fish grease out here. I'm perspiring more than a hen in a fox den. Not to mention these big ass fucking mosquitos are biting like vampires. I see a dark blue SUV pull off the road in front of the house. The tinted window roll halfway down; it was Denise.

"Hi, Quincy, how are you?" She asked.

"I'm fine! How are you?" Shutting off the mower and approaching the vehicle.

"I'm ok. How do you like Evansville? It has changed quite a bit."

"I see. I'm taking a tour of the town after I finish up here."

"Nice, well, take my number just in case you get lost or need something."

"Will do," as I locked her name and number in my phone. "As a matter of fact, Denise. I'm looking for some employment."

Even though I had gotten an excellent severance package and sold my condo, I didn't want to drain my well dry.

"You are an engineer, correct?" she verifies. "Yes, I can fix anything with a motor."

"I might have something for you. Let me make a call, and I'll get back to you."

"That would be a blessing."

"Call me this evening, and I should have some info for you."

"Ok, thank you, Denise; I appreciate you." "No problem Quincy, I'll talk to you later!" Waving as she drives away.

I was walking from the shed after parking the mower, and Terrance pulls up. "What up, cuz! you good, my boy?"

"Man, that shit was wild last night!" Oh yeah, they gave me a solid.

"Boy, you was in that thang powered up! What are you on today?"

"I don't know, probably throw on some clothes and take a ride."

"Come by the house later; you know your Auntie wants to see you."

"What up with that thick ass Spanish chick you had last night?"

"Awe, man, that's my role dawg. We are thick as thieves out chea."

"My bad thought that was your piece."

"Shit, no! I went and hit something else last night, cuz."

"O yeah?"

"Shit chea, I got this slim yella thing across the tracks."

"I heard that. I guess you have to beat them off with a stick, huh?"

"Say Q, you're going to learn these hoes for everybody on the real."

"I don't have time for that. These cats be loose cannons about these women nowadays.

"These females around here play a lot of games, and you fresh meat cuz."

"I hear you, Terrance."

A brand-new Navigator pulls into the driveway. I look to see who it is.

"Shit here comes that begging ass Pastor Taylor!" Terrance groans.

"Afternoon, Fellas! It's a bright sunny glorious day, all praise to jesus the lord our savior." "Man Q, I'm about to get loose before he gets to yapping. I'm going to send you that." He pulls off, kicking up dirt on the pastor's truck, laughing. Knowing he did that shit on purpose. "Terrance, you numbskull!" pumping his fist in the air.

"Hey Quincy, how are you, son!" Dusting himself off.

"Afternoon, Mr. Taylor. How are you?"

"I'm fine, Quincy. I just stopped by to see if you will be joining us on Sunday?"

"Naw, not really my thing, no disrespect." "Oh, I thought since your grandmother was a devoted member, you'd be somewhat interested."

He looked at me as if satan himself was standing in front of him.

"I believe in the universe, Mr. Taylor, but I *would* like to ask you a question." "Go ahead, son."

"Why did the Europeans kill the Indians because they would not accept their god?"

"Son, the lord works in mysterious ways." "I figured you'd say that. So, tell me why the word angel, when spelled backward, is a voodoo evil spirit? Why do they say that Mary was a virgin and married? Last but not least, why do I have to receive my reward in the afterlife when I need it now?"

"You see, Quincy, those are some great questions, but son, nobody can question God!"

"You are right. Unless you are a God." "Now you over there sounding like your

Pawpaw."

"He was a very wise man." He believed in the ways of the Cherokee Indians and felt like we signed a deal with the devil.

"Indeed, he was, Quincy. Well, I have to go; I have lost souls to save. Stop by the house so we can talk more."

"Another time, Mr. Taylor," shaking his hand.

CHAPTER FIVE

While riding through town, Terrance sent me a text about a barbecue he was giving and told me to stop by. I'm not doing anything, plus I need to make an appearance anyhow. Upon arriving at my Aunt Pam's, my dad's oldest sister, I'm taken aback by her big blue and white plantation-style house by the lake. I then spot Terrance in the cut wiping down a clean ass purple old school Chevelle with the same color rims. My cousin is a true Florida boy. He wears long colorful dreads, has a mouth full of gold teeth, and tattoos all over his body.

Looking around, I notice the two women from the spot last night, the sexy slim one and the Spanish woman, standing by the car, smoking, drinking, and dancing to the music.

"What up, Q!" Terrance exclaimed.

"What's happening, cousin!" Embracing one another with a hug.

"Say, cuz these are my people." Referring to the women. Putting her arm around his waist is the Spanish girl. "This is Amber."

"Hey, I most definitely remember you from last night," Amber says, undressing me with her eyes. She then looks at Rose and blurts out, "Bitch, this is the one I was telling you about." staring at my bulge.

Then Rose walks up and puts her arms around his shoulder, displaying a pistol tucked under her t-shirt. "And this is Rose, don't let her looks fool you, cousin!" Terrance says.

"Hey, Cousin! How is your fine ass doing?" Looking at me sexually with her light brown eyes.

Grinning, circling around, checking me out. I felt like a display item. I'm not even going to lie; if they're going, I'm going. These females are sexy as fuck.

"You trying to be kissing cousins?"

The front door opens, saving me from these two hot in the ass women. "Is that my nephew?

Hey, baby, come here and give your Auntie some love." Walking off the porch to hug and kiss me. "There's my baby."

"How are you doing, Auntie? You look great! How have you been?"

"God is good, and I'm blessed! How is your Mama?"

"She's doing good."

"And that brother of mine and your little brother?"

"You already know, Auntie. Daddy is still cussing and fussing, and Charles," shaking my head.

"Like that one over there." Peering at Terrance, we both shook our heads and chuckled.

My other cousin Nicky walks out of the house.

Nicky took a different path than Terrance. Taking her portion of the settlement, their dad left and put herself through college after receiving her Dentistry degree. She went on to open the only black-owned Dentist's office in town.

"Hello, Cousin Quincy!" hugging me tightly. "What's up, Nicky! How are you, cousin?"

"I am great! So, I hear that you moved into Nana's house?"

"Yeah, it needs a lot of work done, but I'll get it right soon enough."

"Yes, don't we know you are Uncle Quincy's son. Mr. Fix it, junior." We both laugh because it's true.

Terrance owns a car wash and a body shop. In the back of the body shop is a full studio, and it's not a bullshit studio either; He's official with his shit. 9 P.M. I received a text from Denise, saying to give her a call. I'm stepping away, calling her from my car.

"Hey, Denise!"

"What's up, Quincy! How are you this evening?"

"I'm well, and yourself?"

"I'm feeling real good, sipping this wine, enjoying the night's skylights."

"I heard that! I have been indulging in some libation myself."

"Well, I have some news for you. I talked to a friend on the council. He's looking for an assistant with engineering experience. Can you meet with him on Monday morning at my office, say around nineish?

"Yes, I can! Most definitely, I'm going to be there suited and booted."

"Great! I will see you then. I will text you the address."

"Once again, Thank you very much, Denise. I will see you Monday morning."

"Looking forward to it!" She says softly. "Good night, Denise! I owe you big time." "Good night, handsome."

Oh yeah, she still wants me, snickering as I'm lighting a square. I'll be swimming in her real soon, saying to myself as I walk towards the front porch.

CHAPTER SIX

Monday morning, I'm up bright and early, putting on my favorite blue suit, a white button-down shirt, and my lucky blue tie; As I'm checking myself out in the mirror. "Watch out, Evansville. Here comes Quincy Palmer Junior Chi-Town's Finest."

I walked into her office at about 8:45 am. "Good morning, my name is Quincy Palmer. I'm here to see Denise Taylor." Her office assistant picks up the phone, "Ms. Taylor, there is a Mr. Quincy Palmer here to see you. Ok," smiling, ending the call. "Please have a seat. She will be with you in a moment."

"Thank you! Sorry I didn't catch your name." Flashing her a smile.

"Hi, I'm Kimberly Maxwell. Denise's Assistant."

"Please to meet you, Kimberly."

"You can call me Kim. Smiling, I remember you. You are Mrs. Palmer's grandson."

"Yes, I am him."

"Well, it was a pleasure seeing you again." "I'm sorry, but I don't remember you."

"I'm Jean's daughter, your Nana's neighbor." "Little Kim, wow, you are grown up!" She's a nice-looking full-figured woman.

"Yes, I have."

The door to her office opens, "Good morning Quincy; We're ready for you." Denise is more beautiful today than when I saw her at the fish fry. That tight-fitting pinstriped skirt and the heels she is wearing got me wanting. Let me stop and focus.

A brown older gentleman is seated on the couch. When I entered the office, standing, he introduces himself, "Good morning, my name is Jimmy Green. I am the owner of Jimmy's luxury sky tours." Extending his hand.

"Good morning, Sir, I am Quincy Palmer Junior," extending my hand.

After some small chat, him and Denise we looking over my resume and a letter of recommendation from Boeing. He is showing me pictures of twin-engine Cessna planes and a helicopter needing maintenance.

He offered me the job and a modest salary even though it was 50 grand less than I was making at Boeing. I accepted his offer. We shook on it like men.

"Great, see you in the morning. We can do your paperwork then." Jimmy implied.

"Thank you, sir. It will be a pleasure to work for you."

Denise and I walked Mr. Green to his car. Waving as he drove off, Denise turns and says. "I'm impressed, Mr. Palmer. You handled yourself quite well in there. You negotiated a twenty thousand dollar raise in an interview."

She said, smiling, batting her eyes at me. "Well, since you are beautiful, as well as kind. Let me take you to lunch?"

"I can do that. Meet me at Joe's Diner at around one o'clock."

"Cool! I will see you at one."

We sit in a booth in the diner to catch up on old times and whatnot. It's a small crowd gathered, and I'm observing the room. We are talking about politics and her dream of what Evansville can become in the future. I admired her charisma; she's extremely passionate about the children and the town as a whole.

"So, tell me, why haven't one of these men snatched you up, making an honest woman out of you?"

"Because the men around here are not motivated to marry." Taking a sip from her glass of water.

"That's a fair answer. What type of man can motivate a woman, such as yourself."

"Seeing the bigger picture. These men here only wants to sleep around and make babies. I'm nobody's side piece or baby mama. I am looking for a man who wants to be his best for me."

"That's not a hard task to ask Denise." I'm smiley-faced, taking a sip of my Root Beer. "What about you? Why haven't none of the Northern women locked you down yet? You are handsome and very well-mannered and pack a big ego if I remember correctly, right?" "Because most of the women I encountered are only concern with showing off a big ring and an extravagant wedding. Not a care about themselves being Goddess."

"So, I take it, you are one of those Pro Black brothers, huh?"

"Naw, you already know, I have my own belief system."

"So, you still don't believe in god or the church?"

"I believe it's a creator, who or what I don't know. I live to be in my higher self always. If someone believes in god or jesus makes them a better person, then who am I to judge?"

Her phone rings, interrupting our conversation; it was her office assistant reminding her of a meeting. "I'm sorry I have to leave in the middle of a great conversation. Maybe we can finish our chat later, you can call me. I should be home around six."

"Will do."

"I feel bad; please let me pay for lunch!" "Now what type of man do you take me for, if I let you pay?" Playfully smiling. "Go on to your meeting. I will call you later."

"Ok, Daddy," she replied jokingly.

"Better watch out now; this is a small town. You know rumors get around quick."

"Bye!" Laughing as she walked towards the exit.

I was checking her out. Like Pac said, putting a little twist in her hips cause she knows I'm watching. She waved as she entered her vehicle.

CHAPTER SEVEN

After leaving the Diner, I swung by Terrance's car wash. My Lac needs to be detailed. All this dirt has my shit looking like I went mud racing. "Look at you, Mr. GQ; where are you coming from, tea in Mar-a- Lago or some shit?" laughing roasting me. "Boy, you look like you going to a bible retreat."

Rose is eavesdropping on our conversation, "You look damn good in a suit. Suits are lingerie for women."

"Shut up. Nobody asked you anything."
"Whatever." Putting up her middle finger.

"Thank you, Rose. No fool, I had an interview with Jimmy. He hired me to fix his planes."

"Congratulations, man, we are going to throw you a party tonight. I'm going to call Amber, time to turn up!"

"Nah! I'm cool on that. I have to get up early." I had to be at Jimmy's at seven in the morning. "For sho. We'll celebrate this weekend."

"Bet, we can do that."

"Rose, get your ass up and stop eye-fucking my cousin! And pull the damn thing in the shop. He ain't got all day to be fucking around with you." Terrance commanded, shaking his head.

Winking at me, "Yes, he does." Taking the sucker out of her mouth.

Got Damn! She is dragging the shit out of that Cornbread, and Collard Green fed ass.

"Say, when is Charles coming down here. I've been watching his videos on the tube; that boy be dripping?"

"I don't know! That boy is doing him."

"I will call him later. I need somebody like him on my team."

"Get at him. He might come if you convince him too."

Later that evening, it was sweltering out, and these damn bugs keep whizzing past my ears. It's like the mosquitoes are attracted to the OFF. I'm rocking back and forth in the chair on the front porch, contemplating calling Denise. I didn't want to seem thirsty, but I wanted to find out more about her.

Fuck it, I'm calling her. Just as I got ready to c all her. My little brother Charles calls.

"I heard you got a job down there," Charles declares.

"Yeah, dad must've told you!" Taking a swig of beer.

"So, you really going to live in that country ass town?" He asked.

"Better than raggedy-ass Englewood!"

"Bro, fuck them bugs, snakes, swamps, and whatever else is in those woods."

"It's not the backwoods dick head. Laughing, they have modern shit down here."

"Fuck that I am a city boy! Please don't tell me they got you in cowboy boots and singing Lil Nas X."

My little brother is funny as hell, always saying something crazy to make me laugh. I was on the phone with him for an hour or so when I received a text from Denise stating she had a great time at lunch and good luck on my first day. Charles interrupted me, "Momma said, when are you coming to get this car out of the driveway?" I had bought a 1990 T-Top Camaro Z28 IROC that I'm restoring. Being laid off allowed me to work on it, and I've put a magnitude of work into it.

The motor is pristine; the old gal just needs some bodywork and a new interior.

"Tell mama I'm flying there in a couple of weeks. You can ride back with me if you want."

I hear rapid gunfire in his background, "What the fuck was that Charles?"

"Some hoe ass dudes, we at war with Trill Ville. They have been smashing shit over here.

They killed little Mike at the G station last night."

"Charles, you need to get your ass out of there. Bring your ass down here and make your music. Your cousin Terrence got a studio here, and he got some nice beats he produced."

"Oh yeah! I might have to come and check it out. What the females look like down there, are they bad?"

"Hell yeah, it is some gorgeous females here. I got my eyes on this one sweet thang right now."

"I bet she got some ass, doesn't she? I know you, Big Bro."

Shaking my head laughing, I swear this boy's brain is fried out, "Get off my phone.

I will talk to you later. I have to work in the morning."

"Ok, tell Terrance to get at me, on the real."
"I got you, holla!"

Laying on the couch scrolling through social media, Denise texts me: "Goodnight. If you're not too tired after work, maybe we can take a walk and finish our chat?"

I text: It's a date. ☺

She texts back. "It's a date! ♡ Call me when you can tomorrow."

Texting: "I will do."

A direct message comes in from social media. It's Rose sending me a friend's request. After accepting it, here comes another message. It's a video of her dancing and getting high in her boy shorts. Rose is persistent. I like her; it's something about her. I send her a picture of my dick print in my boxer briefs. She sends me her cell number. After texting for a while, I got to know her on a deeper level; she's a candid person. We text for a period until I fell asleep.

CHAPTER EIGHT

6:50 a.m. I arrive at work, a little tired; I didn't get much sleep due to how fucking hot it was. The air conditioner is not working properly, of course, amongst other things. I read the online manual for the air conditioner. After work, I'm going to the hardware store to buy parts. I can't sleep one more night in that sweatbox. A gray Chevy pickup truck parks; it's Jimmy.

"Good morning Mr. Green!" Shaking his hand.

"Call me, Jimmy. Calling me, Mr. Green sounds like you talking to my daddy. Come on in here, so we can get to the fun stuff." Taking a sip of his coffee.

"Right behind you," letting him lead the way. While we were working on one of his planes, I noticed Jimmy's hands had started to shake a lot, just like my Paw Paw's use to do. He must have Parkinson's. After I fine-tuned the plane's engines, Jimmy asked if I wanted to learn how to fly a plane. Being the action junky I am, I couldn't say no to an offer like that.

After we landed, "Quincy, you are a natural flyboy. For your first time flying a plane. You learn fast, son."

"Thanks! If I fly a few more times, I can be as good as you."

"Oh yeah, you would. I bet you didn't know I'm also a flight instructor, and you just logged your first hours to becoming a pilot. "Wow! Are you serious? Thank you, Jimmy!" I hugged him like a five-year-old child. I was excited about the opportunity to fly, and this is one of the things I dreamed about doing.

"No need, I need another pilot around here. This 83-year-old body of mine just wants to fish and enjoy my wife."

"How can I repay you?"

"Son, all I want from you is your honesty. I knew your grandmother well, and your daddy too. I know you come from good genes." "Thank you, and I will not disappoint you."

"I know you won't. Or that gal is going to kick your ass!" we both chuckled.

"When you right, you right!" I replied.

"Here are the keys. Go get you some lunch and lock up. I'm going home. I don't have any tours scheduled today."

"Ok, Jimmy, see you tomorrow. I will call you if I need anything." I called Denise to give her the great news.

"Congratulations, Quincy!" Denise Exclaimed.

"Thank you, Denise, appreciate it!"

"How about you come over for dinner around seven? We can celebrate over a bottle of wine!"

"Sounds great. I can do that!"

"Sorry, I have to run. I have a meeting to attend. I'll text you my address." "Ok, have a great meeting." "Thank you. Bye."

Since I came home early, I went ahead and fixed the air conditioner. The house feels like heaven now. I have the O'Jay's blasting, shaving my head and lining up my beard. I then go into my walk-in closet. I pick out a light blue shirt, a pair of khaki-colored crop pants, and my favorite sneakers in the world—the blue and gray air max ones. I'm checking out myself in the mirror. Oh yeah, Now I'm photoshoot fresh.

Before arriving at Denise's place, I make a quick pit stop at the local flower shop.

Walking up to the door, I rang the bell. "Hi!

Welcome to my home!" greeting me with a beautiful smile and a hug as she closes the oak door behind us.

Standing in her foyer, "Hey Denise, these are for you!" giving her an array of colorful flowers.

"Thank you, Quincy; these are beautiful!" The aroma of Asian food hit my nose. "That smells great, Denise. What are you cooking?" "A Cajun-style shrimp and chicken stir-fry with homemade chicken egg rolls. Sorry, I have gotten a late start due to some issues that arose at the city council meeting."

"It's cool, no rush."

"Thank you for understanding; have a seat, please. Would you like a glass of wine?" "Yes, I would love a glass of wine."

As we were sitting at her long, nicely decorated dining table eating, she asked about my day. I told her that I think Jimmy and I will work out well together. She listened attentively, smiling the whole time we talked. Between us chatting, I finished two plates, "That was delicious, Denise, you did your thang on the meal."

"Thanks, yes. It was delicious."

I helped her clean the kitchen; we got on the topic of our love affair we had the last time I was here, you know, the what if's'. Drinking wine; jazz is playing in the background, relaxing on the couch, switching the conversation to the best city in the world: my city, the City of Chicago.

"I have never been to Chicago. I heard they have some lovely landmarks."

"Yes, they do; the skyline is one of a kind. Hey, would you like to go with me next Friday?" "I'd have to check my schedule, but, yes, I would love to go!"

She looks into my eyes, and I gaze back into hers. She has some beautiful eyes; she has a full set of lips that I want to kiss again. But at the same time, I had a weird feeling.

"I will let you know tomorrow. I will look for some cheap flights."

"No! My city, my treat."

A few hours had passed as we were getting reacquainted, I noticed it was getting late. We had already drunk a bottle of wine and was about to open another one. "Well, Denise, as much as I enjoyed the meal and the company of a beautiful woman. I have to call it a night." "I know, right. I have had a long day myself." "Can I use your washroom?"

"Of course, you can," standing up, grabbing my hand, leading me to the washroom.

As I was getting ready to leave, I'm reaching out to hug her. "Good Night, Denise." Catching me off guard, she starts kissing me, pinning me against the wall. I have a handful of her ass as our tongues tussled in a passionate entanglement. She is grabbing at my hard dick, struggling to get my pants unbuckled. My other hand is inside of her shirt, rubbing on her ample breast. She finally pulled him out. I'm turning her around.

A knock at the door interrupts our steamy session. After looking out of the window, I see this stunned expression on Denise's face.

Shit, what the fuck is Derrick doing here! He's supposed to be in Atlanta!

"Quincy, I need you to play this off with me. I will explain later."

"What the hell is going on, Denise?"

"I will explain later." opening the door.

"Hi, Baby, what are you doing here?" hugging the man, pecking him on the lips. A shocked look is across my face as I dipped to the bathroom to assess the situation.

"Hey, Honey! I wanted to surprise you."

I came out of the washroom after fixing myself. "What's up? I'm Q, a friend of the family."

"Hello, Q. I'm Derrick, Denise's boyfriend. I've heard a lot about you. The pleasure is mine."

Who the fuck is this corny ass dude that is speaking on my name! "Good meeting you too, bro. I was just leaving. I'll see you later, Denise; good catching up."

Whatever this is, I am moving around. This is some ratchet shit.

"Likewise, Q, tell Aunt Pam I said Hello." She says as she closes the door, mouthing thank you.

This bitch bogus as fuck. All I could think about as I made my way down the stairs to my truck; was what Terrance said about her. Boy, these women out here ain't shit.

CHAPTER NINE

As I pulled into the garage, I get a call from Rose. "What up, Rose?" I hear loud music and people talking in the background; it sounds like she is at a bar.

"Hey Q, what are you doing?"

"Shit, just getting home. Do you know anyone with some smoke? I need to blow bad." I tried calling Terrance, but he didn't answer.

"I have some. I can come over if you want some company?"

"Yes, slide through. Let me send you my address."

"Boy, I know where your Nana live. I will be there in less than an hour." "Ok, see you in a minute."

I'm sitting on the couch sipping on some 1800, watching Sports Center recap today's action. I hear a knock at the door. It's Rose! I opened the door, I immediately notice how sexy she looks in her short yellow dress and heels, and her face is made up. I have never seen her looking like this.

"Hey."

"What's up. It smells nice in here." referring to the oil from the oil diffuser.

"Where are you coming from all dolled up?" I asked.

"The bar. Tonight, is ladies night." "Does it get packed?"

"Sometimes, that shit is dead though tonight; it's the same ole people."

"Yeah, it be like that, sometimes." Pouring a glass of tequila with a sour look on my face.

"I see you on that 1800 too."

"Shit, the night I had, I need a drink." Wait until Denise shows her face. That shit still has me hot!

"Pour up, Rose; you're my drinking partner tonight."

"Boy, you ain't said nothing but a word. But first, can I use your bathroom?"

Kevin Gates Fly Again is playing on the Bluetooth speaker, while Rose and I are smoking our third blunt. I'm feeling good; you know that point between nice and fucked up. She is there too. I told her about what happened with Denise. Maybe it's the liquor and the smoke taking effect, but I wanted to fuck. I mean, tear down the walls in this house, and the way she is looking at me isn't making it any better. I asked her if she had anything going on with Terrance.

"Hell no! Ew! He's my best friend. We never have and never will." Looking me straight in the eye.

"My bad! Just asking."

"So, what are you saying. You like me now after Denise has done played your ass for a duck?" Passing me the blunt. "I'm not a ratchet ass bitch. I could have told you her ass was dirty."

"Naw, I think you are smarter than you think, different from the women I have met before."

"How?"

"Ever since the first time I saw you. Remember when you punched ole boy. I liked you, you have respect for yourself, and in my world, that's someone you can trust."

No man has ever spoken to her like that. Seen her in that way; either they wanted to fuck or come up. She is digging him, but it wasn't going to be easy. "Q, aren't you just trying to fuck?" Looking at me with this erotic grin, "Stop beating around the bush."

"Yeah, of course, I'm trying to do that; look at you, you are gorgeous, and you're thick as hell!" Rubbing on her tattooed thigh.

"If we do this, I swear on my dead brother's grave. You better not play me."

"The feeling is mutual. I kiss and don't tell, believe that." Leaning in to kiss her.

As we are making out, she stops and says, "Wait, baby. I have to take a quick shower; I've had a long day.

The shower is going the steam from the hot water is fogging up the bathroom. Stepping inside, I see her naked silhouette. Opening the curtain, she turns and gives me a look over. I'm completely naked and aroused.

Handing me the soapy towel, I got in the shower, beginning to wash her tattooed back. She is pressing her body against mine, as I washed away the day from her body. Her hand guided my head toward her neck, and I'm kissing it softly. She let out a sigh. Handing her the towel, she starts cleaning me, stroking my hard-on slowly. "Come here," she commanded, kissing me on the lips.

I'm caressing that bubble ass, rubbing intensely on her puffy clitoris. Her breathing changed; as she pressed my lips to her breast,

I'm licking every inch of her swollen nipple. She moans loudly, "right there; that feels so good." I can feel how moist she is. Whispering in her ear, "I'm going to fuck you like you never been fucked before. I bent her over, and she is looking at me, biting her lip as I slide inside her, grabbing her neck. I'm kissing her as I'm driving this divine rod deep into her abyss.

My hands are spreading apart her ass cheeks, and I'm admiring how creamy she is. Her hands are pressed against the wall, arching her back, giving me the perfect angle to show her my pound game. She squeals with every thrust gripping my wrist. "Yes, right there, baby, you are going to make me explode!" She utters euphorically.

"This is what you wanted, right?" slowing down.

Screaming out, I'm Cumming!" she starts to tremble, her legs are wobbling. "Wait, Q, damn! I wasn't expecting all that." together, we laughed as she is trying to gain her composure.

I carried her to the bedroom; as we lay on the bed, I began kissing on her back, tracing her tattoo of a scorpion on her lower back with my tongue. I'm relishing the taste of her freshly shaven cat. Devouring it like a peach savoring all of her nectar; she clutches my head in satisfaction. Her eyes roll toward the back of her head, and she starts quivering, "Woah!" pushing me off her. I knew I was tearing that ass up,

"Now, bring your ass here and hop on this stick," I demanded her.

"Yes! You want some more of this sweet pussy, don't you?"

"Absolutely," I replied as she slowly slides up and down my pole. She is soaking me in her juices.

"You are hitting my spot baby; I can feel you in my stomach!" She is taking all of me like a champ.

I feel her pussy clamping down on my dick, "Fuck, Rose! I love you." What the fuck did, I just say.

"Awe, Quincy, I love you too!" as a gush of warm liquid covers me. She shouts out, seductively, "Give me that dick!"

I gave her every inch of me, and she was stride for stride, with me. I had sex with many women, but I declare she is the best. I don't know what she did, but our energy was high. "Oh, shit! I'm about to!" Pulling out of her and releasing on her ass, squeezing out every drop. For the first time, I had sex without a condom, and I had an orgasm like never before. I'm perspiring and breathing hard, "Damn,

Rose, that shit was terrific." with a Kool-Aid smile.

Rose laid on top of me, resting her drenched head on my chest, saying, "Boy, you laid down the dick. Like Tony the Tiger, it was great!" rolling over, looking for her purse, "I need a Newport now, and a towel."

I am bringing her a towel and an ice-cold glass of water. Wiping her down as she drinks the water, she kills it, asking for another. We smoked again; afterward, we had sex a couple more times. I was beating the brakes off that thang all night long. Shit, I'm glad Jimmy called, telling me to take the day off. He had to take his wife to the emergency room.

The next afternoon, Rose made breakfast in bed; Honey glazed biscuits, scrambled eggs, and bacon. Just what the doctor ordered, hangover food. I can get used to this. She better watch herself.

"Hey sleepyhead, I'm about to leave. I got clients waiting on me." kissing me. "Call me later." giving herself one last check-over in the mirror.

"Most definitely, I will, sunshine." lightly smacking her on the ass.

Smiling, "You better, punk." walking towards the door. "And thank you, Big Daddy, for the session. I really needed that." Twerking her ass in front of me.

"Come over when you are done at the shop. I'll whip us up something to eat." Not going to lie; I do love her. She is real; a little to handle, but all women are like that; it's a defense mechanism.

Checking my phone, I had missed calls and texts from Denise. Fuck her! She ain't right. As I was enjoying a hot shower, I hear a knock at the door. Dripping wet, I wrap a towel around me. I look out the window before opening the door. It's Denise; what the fuck does this broad want? Opening the door, "What up, fake!"

"Hello Quincy, may I come in to explain what happened last night."

Blocking the door, "Look, I don't need no explanation, Honey." calling her the name ole boy called her.

"I am so sorry for leading you on, but Derrick is not my man; he's a man I have been seeing. He means nothing to me."

"I don't give a shit. You played your hand. Now I'm playing mine."

"Please, give me time to make this right. I want you." Trying to hug me, I pushed her away. "As I said, I don't need shit from you." She is starting to piss me off with this lying ass bullshit.

"I'm sorry if I offended you." With a sad look on her face.

Enough! "I'm good." slamming the door in her face.

CHAPTER TEN

I decided to clean out the old barn and turn it into an auto garage. My phone rang, it's my mother.

"Hey, Ma, what's up?"

She is crying. "They shot my baby! Them motherfuckers shot Charles!" hearing the pain in her voice.

"What the hell, Ma! Is he all right?"

"We don't know yet. We just got to the hospital."

"Ma, I 'm on my way. I'm hopping on the

next flight." I call Terrance for a ride to the airport.

"What up, Q. What's good with it?"

"Man, I need a ride to the airport. Charles got shot."

Stunned by the call, "What the fuck happened?" I just talked to him last night.

Not realizing I just ran a red light, "I don't know shit. My mama just called all hysterical. I got to get to the airport." Fuck! I can't believe this shit. I swear these motherfuckers want me to transform back into my old self. I'm damn near doing the dash, trying to get to the shop. "Say, Cuz I'm going to," Terrance is telling Rose what happened and is explaining to her how to take care of the shop. Terrance goes into the safe in the office, pulling out a bundle of money.

"I don't give a shit. Let's go. I'm bending the block now." Turning the corner like I'm the people, the brakes come to a screeching halt. I hopped out, speed walking into the shop.

Rose runs up to me. "I'm sorry about your brother, baby."

Hugging her tight, I needed her right now. My mother is texting me, saying he is in surgery. Hours later, strolling through the well-lit halls of Christ Hospital, I'm looking for my brother's room. Before arrival, I noticed some detectives standing outside a room at the end of the hall. I knew one of them; we went to high school together.

"What's going on, Monica."

"Hey Quincy, I am so sorry about your brother."

"Thank you, what the hell happened?"

"All I know so far is someone shot Charles during a drive-by on 87th as he got off the exit ramp."

When are these stupid ass motherfuckers going to stop this senseless shooting, "Thanks, Monica, please catch the people responsible for this? Can I go in and see him?"

"Yes, here, Quincy, take my card. Call me when he wakes up, and believe me, I will catch whoever did this."

"Ok, Monica. Thanks again." Looking at her partner as I walked past, looking at me like I'm a suspect.

I talk with the doctor; he explains Charles's condition, "He is a fortunate young man that only one bullet penetrated him. The rest were superficial wounds."

"Thank you, doc." shaking his hand, turning to hug my mother and father.

"Hey, son. we are so glad you made it." "You know, well, I was going to be here, by any means."

We heard a groggy voice say, "I'm going. To the country with you, Quincy."

Surprising us, Charles was awake. "What up, Charles, you scared the hell out of us, little bro."

"Soon, as I'm able to leave here. I'm getting the fuck out of Chicago," turning his head, not realizing our parents were in the room. "Oh, my bad, sorry for cussing."

My mother, with a joyous smile on her face, "It's ok, baby. She kisses him on the forehead. "Charles, God has given you another chance. Please, I'm begging you to leave with your brother."

With tears in his eyes, "I will leave mama, and I'm going to be the biggest rapper this world has ever seen."

"Damn right, you are!"

Terrance chimed in, "Hey auntie Mickey! Hey uncle Quincy," hugging them.

"What up, cousin." speaking to Charles, I got you. I got everything set up. We will take over the rap game." Terrance certified.

"I'm with it, Terrance. I can't keep putting my folk's through this. Q. I love you, Big Bro," he said before the drugs put him back to sleep.

A week later, I finished loading the Camaro onto the trailer. Charles is walking out the door with my mom and dad, with his arm in a sling. My dad walking up to me, "Quincy, watch over my boy, try to keep his ass out of bullshit. Them racists motherfuckers down there will eat him alive."

"I will, Dad, I promise."

"Quincy, drive safe; the lord is with you all. He's watching over everything, making sure you all are safe." She quoted Psalms 23 before hugging me and waving us off as we drove down the street.

"Damn Q, I'm glad we left. Now I can smoke this blunt. Charles says and lights the blunt as we turn the corner.

"Yo high ass. You know your ass not supposed to be smoking and taking painkillers."

"Fuck all that, I need to blow, mix it with these pain meds, shit I ain't got no worries." Charles laughs.

"I'm stopping and getting a Jew town polish before I hit the E-way."

"Good, I can get a pop for this." Pulling out a bottle of cough syrup.

"I swear you a dope fiend!" we both chuckled as he passed me the blunt.

Hitting a bump, "Damn, bro, you did that shit on purpose."

"I thought you didn't have "no worries"?" "Fuck you!" We both are cracking up. "Say little mama, what's up?" Speaking to some chick from the window standing at the bus stop with a body on her, she paid him no mind, "Fuck you then, thot!" as the light turned green.

"Boy, I told you about that shit. No real woman responds to shit like that."

"Get your cornball ass out of here. Captain save-a-hoe; and give me my damn weed back, you hoovering my shit."

We arrived at Maxwell's polish on 95th. Right after I paid for my food, a shootout occurred. I took cover immediately. The little girl standing in line next to me with her mom, was shot in the leg. I'm glad to be leaving Chicago; these cats out here are some predators. I can't wait to get back to the country. I jumped in the car, hit the highway, and got loose.

CHAPTER ELEVEN

In the past few weeks, I have gotten a lot done with the remodeling of the house. I painted inside and out and built a new front porch. I finally finished setting up the auto garage in the barn. Work has been steady at Jimmy's. By next week I will be a licensed pilot. Rose and I are going great. She quit the shop and enrolled in school to become a Nail Technician and a Hairstylist. Charles took her place at the shop. Him and Terrance act like twin brothers, I swear. Both be on straight bullshit. The music is the only thing that keeps him out of trouble.

Charles and I are playing 2k21 on the PS5. I'm getting in his ass.

"You always cheating Q. With Lebron's cry baby ass."

"Boy, whatever, with your Curry shooting half-court shots ass."

My phone rings, and it's Rose. "What's up, Sunshine."

"Hey, daddy, what are you doing?"

"Shit, beating Charles ass on the game. "How is school?"

"I swear I'm going to slap the shit out of this bitch."

"Why?" Laughing because I can visualize her facial expression in my mind.

"Cause this Nestle crunch looking ass bitch keeps stealing my shit," Rose snarled. Laughing enthusiastically, "What she take?" "My flat irons, the bitch is lucky those were my cheap ones." If they were my other ones, this hoe would be picking up her teeth with her ugly fat ass."

"Stop it. I told you, you are too pretty to be fighting."

"Whatever! What do you have planned today?" Rose asked, moving on to another subject.

"I'm going to take Charles to the studio." He's been snapping on Terrance's beats lately. "Ok, cool, I'll fall through there when I leave here. Baby, can I get some dick tonight? My friend is gone." She asked flirtatiously.

"Hell yeah! I have not had any of that cat in

a week." she be tripping, talking about no sex during flow week. Fuck that shit, put a towel down. If man can walk through mud, then I can fuck through blood.

"I'm going to drain daddy's dick dry tonight, I promise." I brought a red sheer nighty; he loves it when I'm in porn star mode.

"It's a sex date then. I will see you at the shop and grab a bottle of Jameson on your way. I like that it is smooth."

"Yes, it is. I will get us a bottle so I can put your ass to sleep." I said jokingly.

"Whatever! More like I'm going to be putting *your* ass to sleep." She retorted.

"Yeah, ok, we're going to see about that tonight, Rose." I rebutted.

On my way to the shop, I see Denise's scandalous ass next to me at the red light. This bitch had the nerve to wave at me. I'm chucking her the deuces and a head nod, we kept pushing.

This bitch has come to my work and keeps texting me, thinking I'm going to give in to her lying ass. Rose has my attention anyway; at least she's been solid with me since day one. Rose wants to beat her ass. Her mama and daddy even tried to convince me to have a sit down with her. Pastor Taylor even tried to threaten my family until my dad checked his ass and sent him on his way.

My mom and dad had come to visit a week later to help me with the house. I laughed my ass off when we ran into Mr. Taylor saw my dad at the gas station. It was like he had seen a ghost.

"Q, isn't that the chick you were telling me about?" Charles asked, looking out the window.

"Hell yeah!" I replied.

"Shit, shorty is bad as hell. You need to smash that since she's trying to go there!" "Man, I ain't got time for two-faced bitches." Real shit, I wouldn't spit on Denise if she were on fire.

"Stop at the store. I need to grab some woods and an ice cup." Charles demanded, signaling me with his finger.

"Look, I have told you, man, I am not your personal Uber."

When we left the blue store, a chick wearing a grey sweatsuit carrying a small plastic bag caught my attention.

"Oh shit, that's Amber," I exclaimed, recognizing her as I got closer.

"Who is that?" Charles asked.

"She is Terrance and Rose's friend," I pulled off to the side of the road.

"What's good, Amber, I almost didn't recognize you with black hair!" Amber usually has her hair colored. "Hey Q, what's up. You know, a bitch just got out of jail." Amber presented.

"Yeah, Rose told me. Your ass is crazy. Why are you fighting the police?"

"Fuck 12! Where are you going?"

"To the shop. Amber, why didn't you have someone pick you up?"

"I don't have their number. The police broke my phone when they arrested me." "Hop in! I will give you a ride."

"Do you have a cigarette? Who is this!" Amber asked, looking at Charles.

"My Little bro from Chicago." handing her a Newport. "Charles, this is Amber, Amber, this is Charles."

"Please to meet you, Miss Lady." Charles has that look in his eyes, *and* he hasn't hit anything since he's been here. I know he's long overdue. "Likewise, cutie." He lights her cigarette as he gets out, letting her sit in the front seat.

At the studio, Charles is in the booth flowing. A thick cloud of weed smoke fills the air. I love being in the studio; the creation of music is impressive, relaxing. I can't explain it, but they're headed in the right direction. Terrance has this white boy named Dave engineering his sessions; he knows what the fuck he is doing. Charles shit sounds live and professional. Some other guys are here, too; I don't know them like that, but these boys are some gorillas. They're over there sipping on lean.

One of the dudes likes to treat his nose, but Terrance trusts them. A tall stinky man walks in. A promotor from Miami wanting to book Terrance for a show. Overhearing their conversation, "I'm saying Tee, if you organize into a label, more doors will open for you." "I'm with that; I'm putting something together."

"You know I got you, Tee. My cousin is an A&R. She is giving deals away like free cheese."

"Bet, you already know, I need that blessing." I hear Terrance respond.

"Nice, get your paperwork together. Who is that in the booth; dude is riding that track?" "That's my cousin from Chicago."

"Shit, there you go right there, you and him. Think about it." Terrance dapped him up and passed him a brown paper brown. Amber walks in; looking casually beautiful, she cleans up well. In her camouflage leggings and a t-shirt that reads 'Chine City' on the front. Charles comes out of the booth at the same time Rose walks in.

"Bitch, when you get out!" Rose blurts, excited to see her.

"This afternoon, Q gave me a ride to the house." she jumps up, hugging her.

"Why you didn't tell me, Q?" Rose looked at me and asked.

"She wanted to surprise you," I explained. "Terrance, I need to power up," Amber says.

"I got you," Terrance replies, pulling out a pickle jar full of orange pills.

Since tomorrow is Sunday, and the Hanger is closed, I decided to partake in the festivities.

A simple gathering at my house turned into a full-fledged party. It seemed like the whole town was here. The sounds of burning rubber interrupted the night's calmness. Terrance and Charles are on the porch having a rap battle. Rose is sitting on my lap while explaining why I don't go to church to a wannabe bible thumper.

"Man, I just told you the bible was written by Europeans that stole the shit from Africans."

"Tell'em, baby; you are so smart." Rose kisses me on the lips.

"See, that is a sin, Brother. You should not be in sexual relations if you're not married." Taking a sip of cold Budweiser, passing me the weed.

"Excuse me! But aren't you fucking the sheriff's daughter?" Rose blurted, stopping him in his tracks.

"That is when my flesh was weak to temptation," he replied, laughing, as he stumbles over his words, trying to think of a lie.

"Bullshit," Rose answered, laughing. "Nigga I caught y'all ass creeping last week. My school is right there by the motel."

"Oh! We were there working on a presentation for the church!" The Bible Thumper replied, with an uncomfortable look on his face.

"At 7:00 in the morning? Ok!" Rolling her eyes, knowing he knows precisely what she's talking about.

"Awe Busted!" I blurted; we all erupted in laughter.

While playing cards, excusing myself to go to the bathroom. Before I opened the door, I hear slapping sounds and moaning coming from Charles's room. I inched the door open, peeking in; Charles was in there having sex with Amber. He was tagging that ass too. He's a true Palmer. I'm not going to lie; I watched for a few seconds, then closed the door and gave him some privacy. I turn around; Terrance is standing right there, scaring the shit out of me. Saying, "Say cuz let me talk to you about something."

"What's up?"

"Q, I have been thinking about forming a record label. I have a good feeling about this shit."

"That's what's up, Terrance!" "I want you to be the CEO!"

That question completely threw me for a loop. I wasn't expecting to be asked anything like that. I never looked at myself as a CEO of anything,

"Man, I don't know shit about the music business."

"Q, look at it like this, you got that mouthpiece; You're the only person I know that can talk to anyone about anything. You got the brains. I handle the music, but I need you to carry me on the business side of things."

"I don't know, Terrance. I'm not comfortable with not knowing."

"Like my daddy always said, sometimes you got to be uncomfortable to get comfortable," Terrance proves.

"True that, cuz! What's the Label's name?"
"Out the Mud!"

To Be Continued...

ACKNOWLEDGMENTS

I want to extend my gratitude to my entire support system. A big thank you to Veenus Publishing for bringing this project to life. I did it! To my greatest inspiration S. L. Vee, thank you for believing in me and cheering me to the finish line. I love you, baby!

To my children, this book is especially for you. An excessively big thank you to my family, brothers from another mother, and friends for loving me and supporting me through this book and life. I love you all!

ABOUT THE AUTHOR

K **areem** is a South Chicago native with a ten- year culinary background, specializing in Caribbean barbeque. He's also the CEO of an independent record label. As a child, Kareem was always good at storytelling, seeing the most intricate of details in almost anything. Seeking a different path for his life and children, he found his way out through words and vision. The ideas and concepts for "Out The Mud" were attained from Chicago's ill-fated streets. The Kareem Kollections takes you on a journey through the expeditions of his out of ordinary viewpoints. His stories are also known for rendering mental visuals, leaving readers craving for the next chapter.

Email: kareemkollections@gmail.com
Instagram: @kareemthewriter
Facebook: @IamKareem
Phone: +708-465-1861
Publishing By: Veenus Publishing ©

www.ingramcontent.com/pod-product-compliance
Lightning Source LLC
Chambersburg PA
CBHW052010170626
46808CB00007B/2867